THE PSYCHOLOGY OF WINNING

"We Always Win"

"I can do all things through Christ who strengthens me."
Philippians 4:13 (NKJV)

CALVIN SCOTT

Printed in the United States of America

First Printing, 2020

ISBN: 9798617850002

Printed in the United States of America

Don Miguel Ruiz Quotes." *BrainyQuote*, Xplore,
www.brainyquote.com/quotes/don_miguel_ruiz_182404.

"Quotes about Familiar." *Quotes about Familiar (552 Quotes)*,
www.quotemaster.org/Familiar.

"Quotes - Eguasch3yahoo.Com (Wilmer, AL) Showing 1-20 of 20." *Goodreads*,
Goodreads, www.goodreads.com/quotes/list/31879372-eguasch3yahoo-com.

"Don Miguel Ruiz Quotes." *BrainyQuote*, Xplore,
www.brainyquote.com/quotes/don_miguel_ruiz_182404.

"A Quote from Releasing You from Fear." *Goodreads*, Goodreads,
www.goodreads.com/quotes/539730-when-your-back-is-to-the-wall-and-you-
are.

Bogue, Robert L. "Use S.M.A.R.T. Goals to Launch Management by Objectives
Plan." *TechRepublic*, TechRepublic, 31 July 2015,
www.techrepublic.com/article/use-smart-goals-to-launch-management-by-
objectives-plan/.

Onherway. "I Do Not Know Anyone Who Has Gotten to the Top without
Hard Work. That Is the Recipe. It Will Not Always Get You to the Top, but It
Will Get You Pretty near." *On Her Way....*, 26 Sept. 2008, onher-
way.tumblr.com/post/51803135/i-do-not-know-anyone-who-has-gotten-to-
the-top.

"When I Was a Young Man I Observed That Nine out of Ten Things I Did
Were Failures. I Didn't Want to Be a Failure, so I Did Ten Times More Work."
Optimize, www.optimize.me/quotes/george-bernard-shaw/18936-when-i-was-
a-young-man-i-observed-that-n/.

"Famous Quotes by Vince Lombardi." *Quotes | Vince Lombardi*, www.vincelombardi.com/quotes.html.

"A Quote from The Principle of the Path." *Goodreads*, Goodreads, www.goodreads.com/quotes/857655-we-don-t-drift-in-good-directions-we-discipline-and-prioritize.

"Perfectionism." *Psychology Today*, Sussex Publishers, www.psychologytoday.com/us/basics/perfectionism.

"One Trick To Get More Work Done Today." *Napkin To Success*, napkintoexit.com/one-trick-to-get-more-work-done-today/.

"Casey Stengel - Quotes and Phrases." *Quote*, quote-citation.com/en/general/4782.

"Katharine Hepburn Art." *Pinterest*, 28 Oct. 2019, www.pinterest.com/eruddell/katharine-hepburn-art/.

"Confidence." *Merriam-Webster*, Merriam-Webster, www.merriam-webster.com/dictionary/confidence.

Philosiblog. "A Man Cannot Be Comfortable without His Own Approval." *Philosiblog*, 18 Nov. 2011, philosiblog.com/2011/11/18/a-man-cannot-be-comfortable-without-his-own-approval/.

"Samuel Johnson Quotes." *BrainyQuote*, Xplore, www.brainyquote.com/quotes/samuel_johnson_122529.

"Joseph Campbell Quotes." *BrainyQuote*, Xplore, www.brainyquote.com/quotes/joseph_campbell_38493.

Angelou, Maya. "An Interview With Maya Angelou." *An Interview With Maya Angelou*, 17 Feb. 2009, www.psychologytoday.com/us/blog/the-guest-room/200902/interview-maya-angelou.

Mowry, Curtis, et al. "Materials Characterization Activities for %E2%80%9CTake Our Sons&Daughters to Work Day%E2%80%9D 2013." 2013, doi:10.2172/1096449.

Jolly, Sanjay. "Ninety Percent Community, 10 Percent Radio." *Strategies for Media Reform*, 2016, pp. 190–198., doi:10.5422/fordham/9780823271641.003.0015.

Bjarnason, Dana, and Michele A. Carter. *Legal and Ethical Issues: to Know, to Reason, to Act*. Saunders, 2009.

"Daniel Goleman Quotes." *BrainyQuote*, Xplore, www.brainyquote.com/quotes/daniel_goleman_285391.

"Health, Help, Happiness + Find a Therapist." *Psychology Today*, Sussex Publishers, www.psychologytoday.com/.

"Walter Anderson Quotes." *BrainyQuote*, Xplore, www.brainyquote.com/quotes/walter_anderson_183075.

Published by Purpose Publishing House
PurposePublishingHouse@gmail.com
www.PurposePublishingHouse.com

DEDICATION

This book is dedicated to all the people who have been in the battle called life. My prayer is you discover the courage to keep fighting as you read the content. I want to thank God for choosing and trusting me to be a change agent in a generation so desperately in need of direction and guidance through some of the most difficult times in the history of mankind. I personally believe my duty and responsibility is to reach this generation.

Calvin Scott

ACKNOWLEDGEMENTS

I want to thank my wife and three daughters for their support and prayers. I want to give kudos to my oldest daughter, Leandra Green, for pushing me to move forward with this project. Thank you for believing in me. I want to thank my mother for teaching me how to survive and overcome, no matter what challenges I may face in life. I would be remiss not to mention Jackie "JP" Phillips of Unheard Media, LLC for her professionalism in helping to establish my brand "Real Talk with the Bishop." Lastly, to my BTWF congregation: You all are the "bomb.com". I am humbled and grateful for your trust in me as your pastor and under-shepherd. All I can say is "To God be all the glory!"

Calvin Scott

TABLE OF CONTENTS

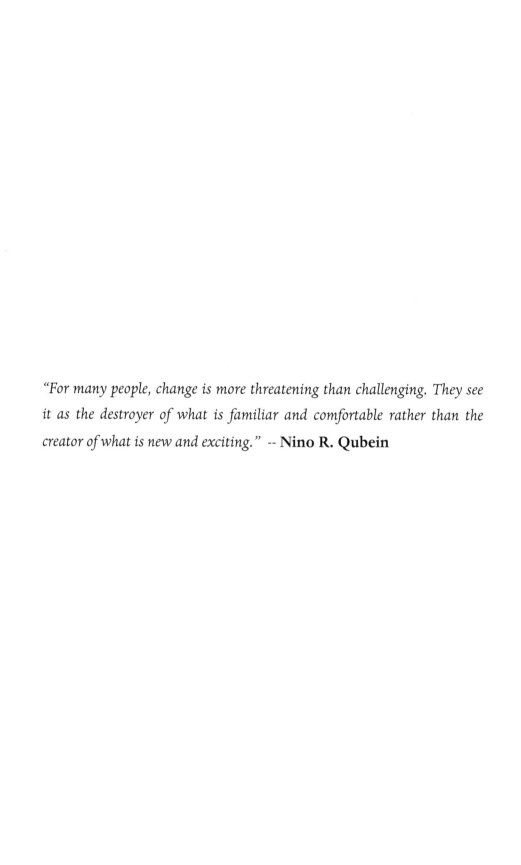

"For many people, change is more threatening than challenging. They see it as the destroyer of what is familiar and comfortable rather than the creator of what is new and exciting." -- **Nino R. Qubein**

FORWARD

We all like to win and yet in this insightful examination of the process of winning, we are mindful that our expectations often assist us in determining if we win or lose. Whether in the spiritual or natural realm, we sometimes win by first losing or succeed after failing. Therefore, our challenge is to continue believing and fortifying an attitude of success so we can achieve greatness even when faced against all odds and impossibilities.

If you've never heard or witnessed Bishop Calvin Scott speak or engage an audience in thinking through difficult theological or intellectual subjects, then you will be blessed by experiencing his gifts articulated with effective and unguarded transparency which illustrates his credibility to affirm how to win over difficult matters.

It is with this approach that we marvel at how he sacrifices himself upon the altar of selfless service as he seeks to encourage, empower, and esteem his listeners; which in this case, are those who turn the pages of this fascinating book.

I've known Bishop Calvin for many years and our journey began long before he was preaching from a pulpit and leading a flock of God. Interestingly though, after much reflection, I must admit that even years ago anyone could see his gift of persuasion and his influence in the lives of people he touched.

He was undeniably a person who believed in winning. During our early days, I was privileged to witness him reveal glimpses of the lessons communicated in this book, especially when we served on the same wrestling team in high school.

It was my task as a novice wrestler to keep Bishop Cavin in shape for his next match. I was assigned by our coaches to press him, challenge his perseverance, and at the same, deepen his discipline and determination not to quit. The point of these challenges was to meet the goal of making him better. During this tedious process, Bishop Calvin was also required to lose weight which at times added pressure to the training process. It was during this season and tough times on the mat that ultimately revealed his internal fortitude and foundational elements for his winning in life.

It took extraordinary focus and a winning mindset to consider victory while struggling through training that only seemed to break you down instead of building you up. Bishop Calvin had to see beyond the present pain and focus his mind and heart on the ultimate plan and purpose of winning, while at the same time, knowing it will sometimes cost you so much.

This book provides valuable life lessons by using a balanced approach of winning mixed with the recipe for hard work and faith blended together. Instructors who tend to massage the mind to believe that we win without exercising action sometimes miss this undeniable truth; however, this book provides a message of faith and works which is wonderfully communicated with practical examples and faithful precision.

While winning, we are reminded that there are no excuses offered to those who want to account themselves as victims. Instead we are encouraged to apply lessons which reveal our true identity in Christ which frees us to no longer accept the victim label, but instead, we are reminded that we are more than conquerors and ultimately victorious.

Our acknowledgement of our true identity helps to create a person with a renewed mind as well as cleanses us from being paralyzed by the past pains and present insecurities. When we know our purpose and that God's destiny is for us to win, we are not slowed by the spirit of fear or kept awake by the nightmare of failure.

Bishop Calvin reminds us that we are always to have a champion mindset and especially while challenged with adversity. It is during these times when the champion inside of us rises to claim his prize.

We are winners because God declares it!

This does not mean we are problem free, but in fact we win by overcoming the problems, obstacles, and challenges that lead us to the victory stand. Moreover, we will win with our arms raised knowing that Jesus has completed the work and finished the race. Therefore, we will continue to believe, work, run and wrestle through knowing that we are winners in mind, body and life!

Bishop Michael F. Jones

THE PSYCHOLOGY
OF WINNING

Winning is not about materialism or simply about sports. It is about life and how we adjust during the battle life affords us all. It's about finding success in your life, on whatever path you take. It may be about finding happiness. It may be about achieving a peaceful mind. It may be about excepting your uniqueness and realizing that God made only one of you out of the approximately seven billion people He created. It is about being successful in the life you desire and working to achieve all your goals. It may be overcoming a nasty divorce or bouncing back from a tragic accident or the loss of a loved one or a dear friend. It may be getting soundness back in your mind back after losing it. Whatever "IT" may be to you, one commonality is winners understand that winning is not a hobby or an extra-curricular activity. It is a mindset and lifestyle. Winners understand, categorically that every area of their lives is impacted by a winning disposition.

Winners may not always succeed at first. Just like everyone else, they may encounter roadblocks along the journey, but their attitude and mindset allow them to come out on top eventually.

They're not independent from the world. Because they see the big picture, they win at home, at work, at hobbies, at church -- basically wherever they go. As a Spirit-filled man of God, I believe my kingdom responsibility is to maintain a winning attitude. It starts with the way a person thinks about themselves. How a person views themselves determines if they will overcome or succeed during life's challenges. Ultimately, God is the source and cornerstone of winning in life.

One of the key building blocks to winning is self-motivation. What is motivation? It is the ability to do what needs to be done without influence from other people or situations. Motivation is what pushes us to achieve our goals, feel more fulfilled, and improve our overall quality of life. It can be described as a reason or cause by which a person or a group of people behave. The cause or reason must be extremely strong, and it often involves self-interest. Motivation is the ability to initiate and persist towards a chosen objective; putting 100 percent of your time, effort, energy, and focus into your goal attainment. It is being able to pursue change in the face of obstacles, boredom, fatigue, stress, and the desire to do other things. It is the determination to resist ingrained and unhealthy patterns and habits. It is doing everything you can to make the changes you want in your life.

Without question, winners in any arena, whether spiritual or secular, must be self-motivated. They must believe they can win at all costs and acknowledge that they are the number-one cheerleader of their destiny. This winner's mindset is derived from one of the two types of motivation: intrinsic or extrinsic. Intrinsic motivation comes from within. Extrinsic motivation is derived from outside sources such as friends, colleagues, religious or spiritual leaders, spouses or children, and so on. Without taking ownership and possessing self-motivation, we will inevitably lose the battle in our minds. It's important to understand that success will never manifest around you until it's established within you. Our attitude or mental state is determined by the dominant thoughts in our minds.

What dominates our life will inevitably rule and control the way we think about and approach life. For example, if sex, drugs, or money dominate our lives, we will spend most of our day chasing it. Life is a compilation of our thoughts; some good, some bad, some ugly. Overcoming negative thoughts without having the right strategy and mindset to win can be very difficult; therefore, we must master self-motivation and recognize it is developed only over time. Self-motivation means maintaining consistent efforts when giving up is easy. It involves doing everything possible to achieve your change goals. Self-motivated people can find reasons and the strength to complete tasks even when challenged. They don't need anyone to encourage them because their desire to press onward comes from within. Self-motivation is the cornerstone to winning. A cornerstone (foundation or setting stone) is the first stone set in the construction of a masonry foundation. It is important because all other stones are set in reference to it. This determines the position of the entire structure. Jesus stated,

"Therefore everyone who hears these words of mine and puts them into practice is like a wise man who built his house on the rock. The rain came down, the streams rose, and the winds blew and beat against that house; yet it did not fall, because it had its foundation on the rock." **Matthew 7:24-26 (NIV)**

As a Christian I have discovered through every season of my life, the only place that keeps me safe and sound is found in Jesus Christ, my savior and hero. He is the Rock!

"I can do all things through Christ who strengthens me." (**Philippians 4:13**)

Self-motivation has many advantages. Self-motivated people, for example, tend to be more organized, have good time- management skills, and more self-esteem and confidence. Daniel Goleman, the author of several seminal books on Emotional Intelligence, identified four elements that make up motivation:

1. Personal drive to achieve; the desire to improve or to meet certain standards.
2. Commitment to personal organizational goals.
3. Initiative, which he defined as the "readiness to act on opportunities".
4. Optimism, which is the ability to keep going and pursue goals in the face of setbacks.

The question is, how hard do you push yourself to get things done? Self-motivation is the force that keeps pushing us to continue, even when we don't feel it. It is our internal drive to achieve, produce, develop, and keep moving forward. With self-motivation, you'll learn and grow – regardless of the specific situation. That's why it's such a fundamental tool for reaching goals, achieving dreams, and succeeding in life. If you don't believe in yourself, you'll be more likely to think, "I knew I couldn't do this!" instead of, "This one failure isn't going to stop me!" Confidence can take a lifetime to build, but only a moment or two to crumble.

It has been studied and scientifically proven that confident people carry a different persona; one of poise, high self-worth, strong discernment between right and wrong, and the ability to lead or convince others to follow. People who are lack confidence are less likely to succeed because they constantly second-guess their ability to do things. They make excuses, often fall short of their own expectations, and fail to meet the perceived expectations of others. Some common excuses people give for not being all they can be are:

"I could never do that because I didn't receive any formal education."

"I'm not cut out for this."

"My Dad never showed me how to do that when I was a kid."

"I'm not even going to try because I know there will be more qualified people applying."

Confidence is knowing. You must know that you are good enough, without blaming anyone else (past, present, or future) for your character flaws. If you haven't done something before, teach yourself how to do it (research). Stop blaming your parents, family, imperfect partner, your kids, etc. Most of all, stop blaming yourself! The power of confidence is a knowing that no matter what you do, you will not fail. I remember my oldest daughter, Elder Leandra Green, encouraged me to start recording live Facebook posts. I thought about my busy life and tried to convince myself that I was too busy. I kept hearing her voice play in my head. Finally, one day I encouraged myself to do it. I didn't realize then that God was using her to motivate and get me out of my self-imposed box to launch out into the deep. Now, I am literally touching thousands of people around the world who follow my ministry.

As an individual, you must make the decision to be a better version of you and take back your life to the Glory of God. Make the decision to take charge of your life and stop making unhealthy life comparisons. Comparison is the thief of joy. It will stall your progress. You can't physically change who you are. You'll always be you and never anyone else.

Make the decision to embrace personal growth and do something you've never done before. Make the decision to stand because you will be in a fight, eventually. No pain; no gain! Progress is not without failure. The only time we fail is when we fall down and stay there. The true measure of success is how many times you can bounce back from failure.

"Under any circumstance, simply do your best, and you will avoid self-judgment, self-abuse, and regret." -- **Miguel Angel Ruiz**

"Never allow your mind to wander untamed like a wild animal that exists on the basis of survival of the fittest. Tame your mind with consistent focus on your goals and desires." -- **Stephen Richards, Think Your way to Success: Let Your Dreams Run Free**

"When your back is to the wall and you are facing fear head on, the only way is forward and through it." -- **Stephen Richards, Releasing You from Fear**

I Am Motivated to Win

In life are internal and external factors that stimulate desire and the energy needed to maintain strong levels of self-motivation. First, self-confidence is the belief in one's own ability; it's self-assurance and a belief in your own ability to succeed. It is an important key to success. Self-confidence is the pre-requisite to success and happiness. It is a combination of a state of mind and a strong feeling of self-belief, which is commonly used when one needs self-assurance -- especially in personal judgment, power, ability, etc. It is that voice which comes from within and gives you a boost to do something you fear.

Today's epoch has no place for those who lack self-confidence because there is no shortage of competition. As believers, we must believe we were born to win, regardless of the odds that sometimes appear to be against us. I see life through one lens: winning. I am not suggesting that we don't suffer defeat or injuries sometimes, whether emotionally or physiologically. I am speaking concerning my thought process and faith in God's ability to bring His word to pass in every area of life. Sometimes people misconstrue having confidence in God with pride or arrogance. As a matter of fact, the devil would rather we submit to a lesser version of ourselves and not walk in our God-given authority. Always remember, as admonished in scripture, we are created in the image of our Creator. God has given us dominion over everything, even our broken past.

The second factor is self-efficacy or the ability to produce the desired result. The essence of this factor is effectiveness. We can't truly be effective if we don't know what we want to achieve. That is why having a vision and goals are so critically important to winning in every area of our lives. Once we determine the strategy to achieve our goals, we must execute. Strategy is deciding what to do. Execution is all about making it happen. We minimize our effectiveness without having a real handle on execution. Execution is the carrying out or putting into effect a plan, order, or course of action. According the Wall Street Journal, "Execution is the single most important trait of a successful person as acting outweighs talking, and successful people not only know that but also live by it every day."

"A lot of organizations put great strategies together, but they don't follow through. Eighty percent of them fail at the execution part of the strategy."

I must confess that I have started projects and fell way short of completion many times. I knew God wanted me to write more books to advance His kingdom and empower this generation; however, I kept putting it off. Sometimes I lacked focus. Other times I was just too busy doing things that did not equate to my assignment. The wheels of progression began to turn when I made up my mind and started writing.

> *"He becomes poor who works with a slack and idle hand, but the hand of the diligent makes rich."* **(Proverb 10:4 AMP)**

> *"The hand of the diligent shall rule, but the slothful will be put to forced labor."* **(Proverb 12:24 AMP)**

The third factor to self-motivation is positive thinking. Your life today is the result of attitudes and past choices.

> *"Your life tomorrow or the future will be the result of your attitudes and the choices you make today."* **(Author Unknown)**

Positive thinking is not the only answer to winning; however, it is a miscalculation not to embrace the fact that our mind is the hub of our thought life. The opposite of a positive thought is a negative thought. You cannot continue depositing both positive and negative thoughts into the same environment and expect success. If you're putting the Word of God into your mental thought process but also entertaining negative, ungodly thoughts, then you might survive, but thriving will be difficult.

"Does a fig tree produce olives, or a grapevine produce figs? No, and you can't draw fresh water from a salty spring." **(James 3:12, NLT)**

The universal law to moving in a different direction is a changed mind. The only effective way to change your life in a positive way is by changing your thoughts and attitudes. We all know, however, it's easier said than done. I can remember numerous times in my life when I struggled to remain positive while being overwhelmed at the same time. Specifically, I recall my earlier years of pastoring. The ministry was thriving with three Sunday morning services and a widely watched television ministry. People were getting saved and delivered. My name and ministry were celebrated throughout the Midwest and they had become a household name. Because of the lives being touched with the Gospel, the devil attempted to thwart the move of God and attacked my home. I had to face one of my worst fears as a father. Not only did one of my teenaged daughters become pregnant, but two were pregnant at the same time. I was on the brink of a nervous breakdown. The weight and responsibility of being the head of my family and leading a church fell on me like a ton of bricks. I found myself fighting depression and feeling a victim of my circumstances. I realized, in that dark season, the keys to winning the battle resided in my trust in God's Word and refocusing my thoughts to see the positive in a negative situation.

The fourth factor to self-motivation is maintaining focus and strong goals. I don't believe you can have the one without the other. Focus is the central point or quality of a clear, visual definition.

It is an idea of the future or a desired result that a person or a group of people envision, plans, and commits to achieve. One of the key aspects of using the mind efficiently is knowing what we want and then concentrating our full attention on it. If we fail to direct our mental focus to the inside, our focus will be distracted by the outside. Instead of "acting," we begin "reacting" to the demands of the outside world.

Strong goal setting helps us to determine our priorities, get organized, make big decisions, and realize our dreams. Goals should be S.M.A.R.T; Specific enough so that we know exactly what we are striving for; Measurable so we can tell exactly when we reach the goal is; Action-oriented to indicate an activity that will produce results; Realistic in that it is practical and can be achieved; and Time- and resources-constrained, meaning it has a definite deadline for completion and realizes limited availability of resources. Your direction is determined through effective goal setting. When you set a goal, you make a promise to yourself. Part of the strength of this is that it gives you a clear direction. Since you've made this promise to yourself, you'll want to keep it.

The last factor to self-motivation is engaging in self-talk. Recognize the role you play in motivating and encouraging yourself. Self-talk is a huge part of what makes us who we are. It impacts how we feel about ourselves, how we feel about what we can achieve in life, how the world views us, and how we interact with others. If you're trying to change your life, listening to your internal dialogue is critically important.

Self-talk can affect your perspective. It can boost you up or take you down. Athletes use positive self-talk to reach their personal bests. Some people use negative self-talk to justify the ruts in which they find themselves. The way you talk to yourself can really impact your confidence. The effect can be good or bad depending on whether self-talk is positive or negative. Staying positive in unavoidable situations is the hallmark of a right kind of attitude (conflict, weakness, getting old, death, betrayal). Self-talk will fall into one of two basic categories: Internal and External Dialogue. In both cases, we talk to ourselves.

Internal dialogue

If you're trying to change your life, it is critically important to look at your internal dialogue. Most of us pay little attention to our thoughts, although we are often controlled by them. Many of us beat ourselves up without even realizing it. It just becomes routine. You will likely never truly feel "great" or love yourself if the internal dialogue is unbecoming. The great thing is negative internal dialogue can be turned around. Being mindful or attentive is where it starts.

External Dialogue

Is it working for or against you? Are you sarcastic, critical, cynical, pessimistic, or hostile? Do you often put others down as well as yourself? Do you call yourself "stupid", an "idiot", or worse when you make a mistake? Are you abusive, cruel, or mean to strangers, pets, or your family when you talk with them or when frustrated?

The way we think and feel about ourselves directly impacts our self-esteem, self-confidence, and self-image. Talking to yourself isn't just normal, it's good for your mental health — if you have the right conversations.

Talking out loud can be an extension of this silent inner talk, caused when a certain motor command is triggered involuntarily. The Swiss psychologist Jean Piaget observed that toddlers begin to control their actions as soon as they start developing language. When approaching a hot surface, the toddler will typically say, "Hot! Hot!" out loud and move away. This kind of behavior can continue into adulthood. Self-talk is important in many ways because it is the script, we use to frame our lives. If we constantly give ourselves negative messages, we begin to develop automatic thoughts that take us from a particular incident to a negative emotional reaction. On the other hand, by filling our mind with the Word of God we can move to positive emotional responses. The way you talk to yourself can really have an impact on your confidence. The effect can be good or bad, depending on whether your self-talk is positive or negative.

"Death and life are in the power of the tongue and those who love it will eat its fruit." (Proverb 18:21, NKJV)

The tongue can bring death or life. What we say to ourselves matters, whether mentally or verbally. What we speak into the atmosphere can have a positive or negative impact on our ability to win in life. If a person constantly speaks negatively over their life, marriage, finances, or career, they will eventually have what they say. I recall as a young athlete in high school or college, whenever I worked out, whether running, wrestling, or playing basketball, I would constantly tell myself, "Mind over matter!" when my body was breaking down from fatigue. I was determined to achieve my goal and not quit because I was getting tired; therefore, I repeatedly said to myself, "Mind over matter," in a rhythmic manner until I finished the task. I would think about the event or game and the fact that I had to be in shape to compete at the highest level of my ability. I knew I had to press past my pain. As a result, I spend more time talking to myself today than anybody else (except God, of course). I constantly tell myself I was born to win no matter how hard or challenging the moment is. Because I am a kingdom man, I believe with God in my life I can overcome any obstacle or challenge.

*"I can do all things through Christ who strengthens me." (**Philippians 4:13**)*

IT'S TIME TO GO TO WORK - THE CONTEST OF THE MIND

2

Two critical are points highlighted in this chapter: the grind of work and the grind of the mind. The word "grind" suggests the ability to withstand hardship or adversity, or the ability to sustain a prolonged stressful effort or activity. It doesn't happen overnight or over the weekend; rather, it is acquired over long periods of time. It is the by-product of perseverance and persistence.

> *"For everyone to whom much is given, from him much will be required; and to whom much has been committed, of him they will ask the more." (Luke 12:48, NKJV)*

It has been said that work is the mother of prosperity. Let's be clear: Inevitable prosperity is equivalent to productivity, and productivity is equivalent to work. Work is defined as an activity involving mental or physical effort done in order to achieve a purpose or result. Work allows purpose to be fulfilled and potential to be maximized. God gives us success and prosperity through productivity. Productivity is something produced because of effort. Those who work hard enjoy the fruit of their labor, which includes countless benefits such as gaining commitment to a task, developing people and conflict resolution skills, self-awareness, gaining personal confidence, and learning to value teamwork. Through hard work, successful people develop good habits for a successful career and future. The ability to develop healthy work habits will determine your earning potential and can impact your effectiveness in society. Healthy habits have a lasting effect on our physical, mental, and emotional well-being. Not only do these habits improve our overall well-being, they also make us feel good.

Healthy habits are hard to develop and often require you to change your mindset. Individuals and habits are all different, so the specifics of diagnosing and adjusting the patterns in our lives differ from person to person and behavior to behavior. For example, giving up smoking cigarettes is different than curbing overeating. This is even different than changing how you communicate with your spouse or how you prioritize tasks at work. Furthermore, each person's habits are driven by their cravings. We pursue that which we crave. pursue. Your life today is essentially the sum of our habits. Our physical health, overall happiness, and success (or lack thereof) are a result of our habits. What we do repeatedly (i.e. what we spend time thinking about and doing daily) ultimately forms the person we become, our beliefs, and the personality we portray.

Developing a reputation for being hard-working and dependable is the key to success. A person's work ethic will often determine the quality and quantity of their rewards. Unfortunately, most people are poor workers. They are unorganized, unfocused, easily distracted, and only work at about 50 percent of their capacity. St. Matthew 25:14-29 gives us a vivid picture of Jesus' perspective of hard work. The parable of the talents outlines the response of the three servants' concepts of work.

> "Their master gave each servant talents, one five, one two and another one. "Again, the Kingdom of Heaven can be illustrated by the story of a man going on a long trip. He called together his servants and entrusted his money to them while he was gone. He gave five bags of silver to one, two bags of silver to another, and one bag of silver to the last dividing it in proportion to their abilities. He then left on his trip." (Matthew 25:14-15)

> "The one with five bags of silver invest his and brought five more, the one with two invest his and brought two more, but the one with one buried his. The two who worked hard and invested the bags of silver received commendation from their master. "Their master to them, 'Well done, good and faithful servant; you were faithful over a few things, I will make you ruler over many things. Enter into the joy of your lord." However, the one who avoided work and received the least responsibility was not commended but condemned for being lazy. "Then the servant with the one bag of silver came and said, Master, I knew you were a harsh man, harvesting crops you didn't plant and gathering crops you didn't cultivate. I was afraid I would lose your money, so I hid it in the earth. Look, here is your money back. But the master replied, You wicked and lazy servant! If you knew I harvested

crops I didn't plant and gathered crops I didn't cultivate, why didn't you deposit my money in the bank? At least I could have gotten some interest on it." (Matthew 25:24-27)

How many times have we allowed excuses or procrastination to dictate our response to ministry, careers, vision, business opportunities, and even failed endeavors? Hard-working people can stay focused and not allow excuses to dictate their decisions. They continually adjust their lenses to ensure prioritization of important goals. The result of hard work equals success. Successful people understand the value of time; therefore they don't waste it on unimportant tasks. With that thought in mind, focus is a critical piece of the puzzle. It requires clarity concerning desired results and the relative priorities needed to achieve specific results.

When I think of focus, I'm reminded of a photographer who adjusts their lens to keep the key subject sharp and at the center of the photograph. They must have a clear and concise perspective of their object. They must have the right type of lens to adjust and capture their subject so the finished product is not distorted or blurred, which requires concentration. Concentration requires the ability to stay with a task until it is completed. Successful people understand that they must work in a straight line to get from where they are to where they want to go without diversions or distractions.

If you want to accomplish your goals, everything you do must take you in that direction. Developing good habits will get you there. This decision alone will dramatically increase the quality and quantity of what you accomplish each day. Soon enough, you will become one of the most successful people you know.

As a husband, father, grandfather, pastor, and community leader, I have had to refocus my priorities many times. I think it is important to re-evaluate our priorities and goals often to ensure that we keep the main thing the main thing. We can get distracted and deterred as results of life situations. Sometimes things are within our control, sometimes they are not. Whatever the case or circumstance, anyone not willing to work diligently will decrease their potential significantly.

Our Creator has purposed for the man to work. Unfortunately, because of man's fallen nature, work is seen as a hinderance to success and not a benefit. God's purpose for work has several reasons:

1. It is God's tool to help men to be productive and fruitful.
2. Work is God's inherent gift to help men to discover their potential.
3. For a man, his work brings forth the possibilities that will die with him unless they are activated, performed, produced, and fulfilled.
4. Work releases potential and empowers success. Laziness, which is the absence of work, aborts potential and sacrifices possibilities.
5. God works the vision in; man works the vision out.

I am amazed when I think about all the times I toiled to bring different visions to pass in my life. I'm equally stunned by the number of times I felt like giving up. During those times I was awakened to the reality of no pain- no gain. The grind of work is the grind of life.

> "Diligent hands will rule, but laziness ends in slave labor..." (**Proverbs 12:24, NIV**)

> "Do you see a man who excels in his work? He will stand before kings; He will not stand before unknown men." (**Proverbs 22:29, NKJV**)

> "He who is loose and slack in his work is brother to him who is a destroyer and he who does not use his endeavors to heal himself is brother to him who commits suicide." (**Proverbs 18:9, AMP**)

> "I do not know anyone who has gotten to the top without hard work. That is the recipe. It will not always get you to the top, but it will get you pretty near." -- **Margaret Thatcher**

> "When I was a young man, I observed that nine out of ten things I did were failures. I didn't want to be a failure, so I did ten times more work." --**George Bernard Shaw**

"The Contest of the Mind – Developing Mental Toughness"

The goal of winners in Christ should be to connect hard work with mental toughness. You cannot have true success in Christ without hard work and mental toughness. The question becomes what role does mental toughness or the grind of the mind play in winning?

To begin, mental toughness is the ability to resist, manage, and overcome doubts, worries, concerns, and circumstances that prevent you from succeeding. Mental toughness allows you to excel at a task, towards an objective or a performance outcome that you set out to achieve. It's having the resilience or an ability to recover quickly, bouncing back from setbacks and failures; spotting and seizing opportunities with confidence. Mentally tough people set themselves apart from the crowd. Where others see impenetrable barriers, they see challenges to overcome.

Thomas Edison failed 1,000 times before creating the lightbulb. Although the exact number of tries has been debated (ranging from 1,000 to 10,000 attempts), it's safe to say Edison tried and failed a lot before he successfully created his beacon of light. His response to repeated failures? "I have not failed. I've just found 10,000 ways that won't work." Ironically, when Thomas Edison's factory burned to the ground in 1914, destroying one-of-a-kind prototypes and causing $23 million in damage, his response was simple, "Thank goodness all our mistakes were burned up. Now we can start fresh again."

Albert Einstein didn't have the best childhood. He didn't actually speak until he was four years old. In fact, many people thought he was just a dud. Throughout elementary school, many of his teachers thought he was lazy and wouldn't make anything of himself. He always received good marks, but his head was in the clouds, conjuring up abstract questions people couldn't understand. He continued thinking and eventually developed the theory of relativity, which many of us still can't wrap our heads around.

Benjamin Franklin dropped out of school because his parents could only afford to keep him in school until his tenth birthday. That didn't stop the great man from pursuing his education. He taught himself through voracious reading and in time, he invented the lightning rod and bifocals.

Oprah Winfrey gave birth at age 14 and lost her child. She is one of the most successful and richest people in the world today, but her life hasn't always been so easy. She grew up in Milwaukee, WI and was repeatedly molested by a cousin, uncle, and family friend. Eventually, she ran away from home, and at age 14 gave birth to a baby boy who died shortly after. Winfrey's tragic past didn't stop her from becoming the force she is today. In high school she excelled as an honors student and won an oratory contest, which secured her a full scholarship to Tennessee State University. Now the entrepreneur and personality has the admiration of millions and a net worth of $2.9 billion. Nelson Mandela worked hard to train as a lawyer, despite South African apartheid, which made life difficult for black men. It's amazing that he survived 27 years in prison. He was a South African anti-apartheid revolutionary, politician, and philanthropist who served as President of South Africa from 1994 to 1999. He was the country's first black head of state and the first to be elected in a fully representative democratic election.

The Bible tells us that at the age of seventeen, Joseph was sold into slavery. At thirty, he became the prime minister of Egypt. He survived years of rejection by his family. During one of the worst famines in Egypt's history, he became a conduit of survival for his family. Through his powerful position of influence, God strategically used him to be in the right place at the right time to bring His Word to pass.

The common denominator in all these instances is mental toughness. Of course, I would be remiss not to give God His due honor for giving us the ability to have mental toughness. Without question, He is the source of everything. By His unmerited grace, all of us are given the privilege and opportunity to become great. The Bible states:

> *"For by grace you have been saved through faith, and that not of yourselves; it is the gift of God, not of works, lest anyone should boast. For we are His workmanship, created in Christ Jesus for good works, which God prepared beforehand that we should walk in them." (Ephesians 2:8-10, NKJV)*

> *"Therefore, prepare your minds for action; be self-controlled; set your hope fully on the grace to be given you when Jesus Christ is revealed." (1 Peter 1:13, NIV)*

> *The Apostle Peter states, "Therefore, prepare your minds for action; be self-controlled; set your hope fully on the grace to be given you when Jesus Christ is revealed." (1 Peter 1:13, NIV)*

"Mental toughness is many different things and rather difficult to explain. Its qualities are sacrifice and self-denial. Also, most importantly, it is combined with a perfectly disciplined will that refuse to give in. It's a state of mind – you could call it character in action."-- **Vince Lombardi, legendary NFL football player and head coach**

Mentally tough people are flexible and constantly adapting. They know that the fear of change is paralyzing and a major threat to their success and happiness. We are bound to fail when we keep doing the same things we always have in the hope that ignoring change will make it go away. It's exponentially easier to create an identity from the things we have experienced, (the external) rather than the core part of who we are (the internal). We lose touch with the vast possibilities within because we're used to our little story. When our story becomes our identity, we dampen new sparks of change because they don't fit with our past. Whatever you're used to becomes the default mode in your life. If you're used to feeling disappointed, unattractive, not smart enough, or financially incapacitated, those feelings stick with you. Mental toughness is needed to take us from our past into our future.

"I beseech you therefore, brethren, by the mercies of God, that you present your bodies a living sacrifice, holy, acceptable to God, which is your reasonable service. 2 And do not be conformed to this world, but be transformed by the renewing of your mind, that you may prove what is that good and acceptable and perfect will of God." **(Romans 12:1-2)**

For us to maintain the right mental perspective, perseverance becomes the fuel by which a steadfast effort to follow God's command and do His will is sustained in every situation. Faith alone can save; however, it's equally clear that perseverance while doing good works is the greatest indication that an individual's faith is genuine. Perseverance springs from a faithful trust that God has been steadfast toward His people. Through persevering in God's work, Christians prove their deep appreciation for God's saving grace.

> *"Therefore, my dear brothers, stand firm. Let nothing move you. Always give yourselves fully to the work of the Lord, because you know that your labor in the Lord is not in vain."* **(1 Corinthians 15:58, NIV)**

Our mentality has a powerful effect on our ability to succeed Let's be honest, maintaining the right mental disposition can be very difficult when your reality is overwhelming and crushing. I remember in 2015 when my wife and I went through a very difficult season in our marriage. I found myself, after 35 years of marriage, with no hope of things ever changing in our relationship. After much prayer and counsel, I filed for a divorce. I am not suggesting that was the right thing to do; however, when your hope is gone, maintaining a Godly perspective over long periods of time is very difficult

In my estimation, this was the most mentally challenging time of my life. During the process, my wife and I had to live through lies, rumors, and attacks on our character. To further intensify this difficult season, my pastoral mantle was brought into question by very judgmental and condemning "church" people. I learned many things about my confidence and trust in the Lord and people. I expected some betrayal; however, what crushed me emotionally was the betrayal I experienced by people I least expected. This was a tsunami of a test, but I remained faithful to the call of ministry while battling a war in my mind. I found myself, on numerous occasions, on the brink of a nervous breakdown. I was leading while bleeding! I also gave serious consideration to resigning as the senior pastor. During this season, I discovered a level of mental toughness and the grind of the mind I would have never realized without God's help. My faith deepened further, and I believed God would work things out for my good and His glory. I find thinking about how God will permit us to face some of the most difficult seasons in our lives and at the same time, build our capacity to believe Him at another level to be interesting. To God be all the glory, my wife I survived. I believe when God is the center of your world, He will carry you through life's ups and downs.

The Grind of the Mind

The grind of the mind is synonymous to a disciplined mind. Note, discipline is not something you have or don't have; nor is it something you're born with. It is a decision you make to do something and complete it. It could also be a decision not to do something. A disciplinary action refers to one's self-control to conform to organizational rules and regulations. Discipline is completing every task in the present time frame. It is balancing body, soul, and spirit. It is the ability to stay focused and on course. Discipline is always keeping the commitments we make with ourselves and others. It is the determination to keep going when the going is tough. It is being on time every time.

"For a moment, all discipline seems painful rather than pleasant, but later it yields the peaceful fruit of righteousness to those who have been trained by it." **Hebrews 12:11 (ESV)**

Remember the following truths:

- A discipline mind is a focused mind.
- A disciplined mind can get things done.
- A disciplined mind is action-oriented.
- A disciplined mind is focused on progress.
- A disciplined mind can focus on a subject and improve consistently.
- A disciplined mind is sharp.

"We don't drift in good directions. We discipline and prioritize ourselves there." – **Andy Stanley**

When you think of Unwavering Discipline, what comes to mind? We must all suffer one of two things: the pain of discipline or the pain of regret." – **Jim Rohn**

DEFEATING THE GIANTS OF "THE FEAR OF FAILURE" AND "REJECTION"

3

We all are forced to confront giants in our lives. Avoiding them is impossible. The word "giant" is a metaphor for seemingly insurmountable situations or problems. Job 14:1 (TLB)

states, "How frail is man, how few his days, how full of trouble!" Job's life proves that we are going to have an abundance of challenges in life. Certainly, he was an expert on adversity and problems. He faced the fear of failure and rejection. He lost all ten of his children and wealth in one day. His wife and friends betrayed him during the most difficult period in his life. When we feel insecure or unsafe during times of uncertainty, a natural response is to become fearful.

Fear is an emotion. It is generally induced when the subject perceives a threat. Phobia is the Greek word for "' fear", and it can be defined as the "excessive or unreasonable fear of an object, place, or situation." Often, what we fear the most comes to pass more speedily than what we hope. Fear is our response to two kinds of threats: real and imagined. You already know the difference. Real threats pose a risk to our survival. Imagined threats are hypothetical scenarios. Delivering a speech in front of a group of people is an imagined threat because it has little risk to your survival. Delivering a speech in front of a pack of lions in the African wilderness is a real threat because of the audience. They would be more interested in eating you than hearing you.

Fear of failure involves imagined threats. While the fear is real, the threat is not. For the time being, the threat is a prediction, a product of your imagination, a scenario built in the mind. This doesn't make your fear unfounded or irrational, but rather premature and unnecessary. Instead of letting fear stop you, study it. Plan how to conquer it. Change your mind to embraces of overcoming the fear. Envision a achieving your expected goal.

I am a golf enthusiast. I love playing the game for several reasons. First, it's a very mentally challenging sport. Secondly, in my opinion, it's a metaphor for life. It challenges your integrity and honesty. The thought is if you cheat in golf, you will cheat in life. Unlike most sports which have team members who assist on the field or court, golfers are loners. No one is there to block or pass the ball to you. The competition is strictly against you and the golf course. For many golfers, hitting the ball into the water is a constant fear, particularly when the water is directly between them and the green. I discovered in order to overcome that fear, I had to focus on the goal; the end result. Obviously, I realized if I lose the battle with fear in my mind, then I lose the battle in the moment.

Perhaps golf is not your battle ground. Regardless of the sport, activity, or venue, the perspective is the same. I don't believe anyone goes to battle with an intent to lose. Likewise, no one gets married with the intent to divorce or start a business to go out of business. If a person allows the fear of failure to paralyze them during difficult times, it is highly unlikely they will win or overcome the obstacles standing between them and their desired end.

What is failure? Giving up? Never going after your goals? Not achieving a desired outcome? You may think that the answer is obvious; however, failure is subjective and perceived individually. Failure could be perceived as the looming potential of your marriage ending in divorce, the collapse of your business or, as a pastor, the reality of losing your ministry. A parent may experience feelings of failure as their child suffers from a chronic disease that could possibly end their life. Perhaps you set a goal to lose weight and fell short of your target. Whatever life event you encountered, failure can only be defined individually.

Failure is defined as a lack of success or something that falls short of what is required or expected. It is important to be clear about what we consider failure, since failure is the object of our fear and an obstacle to our success. It's almost impossible to live without experiencing some kind of failure. People who do probably live so cautiously that they go nowhere. Put simply, they're not really living at all. Having a clear understanding of failure is important. Every time we fail at something, we can choose to look for a lesson to learn or be swallowed up in discouragement and depression. These lessons are important, as they help us to grow and prevent us from repeating the same mistakes. Failures stop us only if we let them.

Finding successful people who have experienced failure is easy. For example, Michael Jordan is widely considered to be one of the greatest basketball players of all time. And yet, he was cut from his high school basketball team because his coach didn't think he had enough skill. Warren Buffet, one of the world's richest and most successful businessmen, was rejected by Harvard University. Richard Branson, owner of the Virgin empire, is a high-school dropout. Imagine if Richard Branson had listened to the people who told him he'd never do anything worthwhile without a high-school diploma.

In life, most of us will stumble and fall. Doors will get slammed in our faces, and we will also make some bad decisions. Imagine if Michael Jordan had given up on his dream to play basketball when he was cut from that team. What if he had quit instead of overcoming the fear of failure? Because of his commitment to winning, he won on the court, leading the Chicago Bulls to six NBA Championships and off the court, securing millions of dollars in endorsements and business deals. Think of the opportunities you'll miss if you let failure stop you.

Failure can also teach us things about ourselves that we would not have learned otherwise. For instance, failure can help you discover your strengths. Failing will help you discover and identify your truest friends. Through failing, often you can find an unexpected motivation to succeed. Valuable insights come only after a failure. Accepting and learning from those insights is key to succeeding in life. Finding the benefits of past failures is monumental to winning.

"The Fear of Failure" is being afraid of not accomplishing a desired goal. Often, this fear can cause people to sabotage their own efforts to avoid the possibility of a bigger failure. Fear of failure is a significant obstacle that stands between you and your goals; but it doesn't have to be. It is the intense worry you experience when you imagine all the horrible things that could happen if you fell short of achieving a goal. The intense worry increases the odds of you holding back or giving up. Being successful relies, to a large extent, on your ability to leverage fear. To make your goal pursuit fail-proof, switch from thinking about failing to winning. Don't allow fear to cause a discrepancy between what you hope to achieve and the actual outcome. What is standing between you winning or achieving your goals? What mental impediment has engulfed your mind? What is standing in the way of you conquering your fears?

All negative experiences have some benefits, even if they are hard to see or appreciate in the moment. Finding the benefits of past failures requires practice, but you can master and enhance this ability so that it becomes second nature. This is something I've personally experienced. I never really considered myself a successful businessman. I made some money, but it was never to the degree I thought it should have been. I purchased a tax franchise and even a Chuckie Cheese-type business called BT's Party Center. Thousands of dollars were invested in hiring employees and purchasing equipment and supplies, which included inflatables and video games. I even paid for an employee to travel to Dallas for formal training to learn how to manage the business. It was a great concept, but unfortunately, the business failed.

I had every opportunity to allow the fear of failure to control my destiny. Instead, I reminded myself that God clearly tells us all things work together for our good and for His glory. I learned, that when I don't achieve a particular goal, to extract what part of the opportunity can be used as a teachable moment. I use that positive approach to build on. It keeps me from allowing defeat and failure to completely control my response in the moment. It is important to constantly remind yourself that life is a marathon and not a sprint when it knocks you down. Maybe you didn't reach a desired goal; perhaps the business or relationship failed. Whatever the case, it doesn't make you a failure. We all get knocked down sometimes, just don't stay there.

The key to winning in any arena is not suppressing fear, but managing and channeling it in the right direction to accomplish the task at hand. David confronted and defeated a Philistine champion giant by the name Goliath. When all of Israel was petrified by the reputation of this massive giant, David was able to defeat him with a sling and a rock. He was not afraid because he remembered the many times God had given him the victory over the giants in his past. He was not afraid of Goliath. The greatest hindrance to faith and winning the contest is not the absence of God's power, but fear.

"For God has not given us a spirit of fear, but of power and of love and of a sound mind." (2 Tim 1:7 NKJV)

I am pretty sure no one wants to lose in an athletic contest, competing for a business contract, or pursuing a degree in school; however, we all know in a competition someone will win or lose. Champions never become comfortable with losing. They know the fear of failure looms in any competitive arena. They know the potential of losing is minimized if they believe they can win. The Lord gave the children of Israel the promise land, but some giants were already occupying the land. Joshua and Caleb believed they could conquer them The other ten spies, however, were filled with the fear, so the perspective of their report contradicted that of Joshua and Caleb. Their self-perspective was flawed and based on what they saw more than what God promised.

"Then Caleb quieted the people before Moses, and said, "Let us go up at once and take possession, for we are well able to overcome it But the men who had gone up with him said, "We are not able to go up against the people, for they are stronger than we." And they gave the children of Israel a bad report of the land which they had spied out, saying, "The land through which we have gone as spies is a land that devours its inhabitants, and all the people whom we saw in it are men of great stature. There we saw the giants (the descendants of Anak

came from the giants); and we were like grasshoppers in our own sight, and so we were in their sight." (Numbers 13:30-33)

The way we see ourselves has a direct impact on how we respond to life's opportunities. Ten of the spies saw themselves as grasshoppers and only two saw themselves as God saw them. We were created by God the win in every area of our lives. Winning starts in the heart and head. The heart and the head work in concert with the will God has for our lives. Many people are afraid of failing, but the fear of failure crosses the line when it becomes debilitating. It can render us immobile, preventing us from moving forward.

How many times have we allowed ourselves to be paralyzed by the fear of failure and rejection? According to Psychology Today, three characteristics contribute to the fear of failure and rejection: People-pleasing, Perfectionism, and Pessimism. People-pleasing is simply the fear of man. Psychology Today states:

"Many people-pleasers confuse pleasing people with kindness. When discussing their reluctance to turn down someone's request for a favor, they say things like, "I don't want to be selfish," or "I just want to be a good person." Consequently, they allow others to take advantage of them. People-pleasing can be a serious problem, and it's a hard habit to break."

The fear of appearing as a failure to others controls and confines a person's thoughts and actions. In scripture, Solomon admonishes this consideration:

"The fear of man brings a snare, but whoever trusts in the Lord shall be safe." (Proverb 29:25).

Perfectionism, on the other hand, is pride at its core. It refuses to accept any standard lower than perfection. People with this mentality set excessively high standards, strive for flawlessness, and are overly critical of themselves and others who fail to reach their standards. Fear of failing due to perfectionism renders a person useless. This, too, is a snare because God's Word tells us *"for all have sinned and fall short of the glory of God"* (**Romans 3:23**). All of us have something we are working on daily. There is always a battle between our mind and reality with which we have to contend.

Finally, Pessimism is fearing that whatever is hoped for will not happen. There is no confidence in the future. Pessimists look at challenges with a "glass-half-empty" mentality. They refuse to believe the best and eliminate any positive expectations. This is a serious problem because it comes from within the heart. The Psalmist cries out to himself, *"Why are you cast down, O my soul, and why are you in turmoil within me?"* (**Psalm 42:5**). His faith wrestles with his fear. I must re-emphasize that the fear of failure and rejection, in my humble opinion, is the root cause of not winning in life. We must remember, if God is for us, who can be against us!

I encountered many pessimists in my early years of ministry. When I first started my church, with no money or support, many people thought it wasn't going to survive. People rumored that I wasn't going to make it, as some said I was full of pride. I can remember the Lord speaking to me one Wednesday night as I was leaving the church. He said, "You are a trailblazer and have an "Apostolic Anointing" on your life. Because of this, you are going to face much reproach." In other words, the Lord was confirming my ministry call as a trendsetter and affirming my position in the kingdom. I am grateful I did not listen to the report of negative people and their perspective of my destiny. All I can say is God has proven Himself to me in ways I would have never experienced if I allowed fear and rejection to rule my faith in God.

The Fear of Rejection

"The Fear of Rejection" is one of our deepest human fears. Biologically, we are wired with an innate desire to belong. We fear being seen in a critical way and tend to be anxious about the prospect of being cut off, demeaned, or isolated. We fear being alone. Feeling rejected hurts. It undermines our confidence and makes us doubt our worth. Whether you've experienced this once or twice in life, or whether a common occurrence, it can lead to a deep anxiety about future rejection. Trapped by a horrible feeling of worthlessness, we might let our fear of rejection stop us from even trying to pursue and achieve our dreams. This makes us feel worse about ourselves, creating a vicious cycle of fear and, oftentimes, low esteem. Before we know it, a sense of hopelessness can set in, especially when we feel like we've tried everything we can to improve. We begin to see life through the lens of the fear of rejection and once rejection gets a grip, we find ourselves struggling in the swamp of fear and discouragement.

Rejection is the most common emotional wound sustain in life. Our risk of rejection used to be limited by the size of our immediate social circle or dating pools. Today, thanks to electronic communications, social media platforms, and dating apps, each of us is connected to thousands of people. Any of them might ignore our posts, chats, texts, or dating profiles, and as a result we are left feeling rejected. Millennials, unfortunately, base the bulk of their response to life on how people view them more than any other generation in the history of creation. In addition to these seemingly minor rejections, we are still vulnerable to more serious and devastating rejections. When our spouse leaves or betrays us, when we get fired or laid off from our jobs, snubbed by our friends, or ostracized by our families, the pain we feel can be absolutely paralyzing. Not to mention, the betrayal of a fellowship Christian can leave one staggering, trying to figure out how to trust people again. Whether the rejection we experience is large or small, one thing remains constant: It always hurts, and the hurt is usually more than we expect. One writer stated,

> *"The greatest damage rejection causes is usually self-inflicted. Just when our self-esteem is hurting most, we go and damage it even further."*

Rejection affects us psychologically and emotionally. It causes pain in both areas. Rejection damage our mood and self-esteem. It elicit swells of anger and aggression destabilizes our need to "belong. Unfortunately, the greatest damage rejection causes is usually self-inflicted. Indeed, our natural response to getting picked last for a team or looked over for a promotion in the workplace is not just to lick our wounds, but to become intensely critical of ourselves. We call ourselves names, lament our shortcomings, and feel disgusted with ourselves. In other words, just when our self-esteem is hurting most, we damage it even further. Doing so is emotionally unhealthy and psychologically self-destructive, yet every single one of us has done it at one time or another.

I remember quite vividly during my 25th high school class reunion, different people were taking group pictures of various members. Everyone was excited to see each other. The atmosphere was filled with enthusiasm. One incident that was quite painful and embarrassing for me was the open rejection by one of my male classmates. We gathered to take a group photo, which was the pattern of the evening, As all the male classmates stood together in preparation of the photo, a particular classmate abruptly asked me to get out of the picture. I was shocked, as I never anticipated that curveball. I began to immediately ask myself what I did to deserve this mistreatment and rejection by a person with whom I thought I had a decent relationship. As I tried to think of a situation or incident that might have happened in the past, I found no justification for his dislike towards me. I had to regroup emotionally and psychologically. Quite candidly, I was emotionally distraught. The other guys were just as shocked as me. In that moment, I had to remind myself of who I was in Christ, be strong, and not allow that incident to define me. To God be the glory, I didn't even hold a grudge against my classmate. I figured whatever the problem he had with me was not my problem. One thing is for sure, when it comes to winning the battle over the fear of rejection, we cannot win if we don't believe in ourselves and the God who created us in His image. He has given us dominion over everything, which includes fear and rejection.

"For God has not given us a spirit of fear and timidity, but of power, love, and self-discipline. (2 Tim 1:7, NLT) I can do all things through Christ who strengthens me." **(Philippians 4:13, NKJV)**

OVERCOMING THE VICTIM'S MENTALITY

4

The victim's mentality is a personality trait in which a person tends to recognize themselves as a victim of other people's negative actions. They behave as if this were the case in every situation. It is a *learned* and *acquired* behavior, which means it does not have any biological or genetic workings at its base.

The victim's mentality depends on clear thought processes and attribution. It's something that the person has brought on due to constant churning and spinning of negative thoughts. The victim believes they have been wronged. In the true sense of the word, a victim is described as someone who has been harmed even though they were not responsible for the incident, could not prevent the same, and, therefore, deserves empathy. In many instances, people who have a victim's mentality are under the impression that they have been treated unfairly and wronged without any fault of their own, even though in some cases evidence clearly proves that they were responsible (completely or partially) for what happened.

The Bible speaks of a man who had an infirmity for 38 years (St. John 5:1-8). The most unfortunate thing is he submitted himself to his condition. Over time, in his mind he saw himself as a victim of his circumstance. When we read the text, Jesus never addressed his reasons or excuses for not getting in the pool of Bethesda when the water was stirred. He simply asked him, "Do you want to be made whole?" In other words, I know about the circumstances and how long you have been dealing with them. One thing is for sure, the longer we feed our mind with defeated communication, inevitably we will fall prey to thinking like a loser. By accepting his condition for so long, this guy imprisoned himself mentally and submitted to a lessor version of himself.

To further validate my point, the victim believes they have no control over life situations and their outcomes, and, therefore, shed responsibility. When faced with negativity or setbacks in life, they refuse to do anything about it and move on; instead, they focus on the negative and repeatedly meditate on it, and thrive on the drama. This leads them to believe in the worst-case scenario.

People who adopt a victim's mentality are a classic example of pessimists. They look at every situation as a potential wet blanket. They feel that the world is out to get them, even though there might be evidence indicating otherwise. They are the first ones to point out the possible negative outcomes of any new situation and refuse to try something new themselves, but also discourage others with their constant negativity. This leads to people consistently being guided by unhealthy emotions like anger, fear, and sadness.

The intentions of people always come with suspicion. In Exodus chapter 14, we read about how God gave the children of Israel

THE PSYCHOLOGY OF WINNING

victory over Pharaoh and the Egyptians. From this point, the Israel-
ites went three days in the wilderness without finding water until
they came to Marah, where the water was so bitter that they could
not drink it. I find it interesting, however, that Israel forgot about
God's divine providence when they became thirsty.

> "So, Moses brought Israel from the Red Sea; then they went out into
> the Wilderness of Shur. And they went three days in the wilderness
> and found no water. Now when they came to Marah, they could not
> drink the waters of Marah, for they were bitter. Therefore, the name
> of it was called Marah. And the people complained against Moses,
> saying, 'What shall we drink?' So, he cried out to the Lord, and the
> Lord showed him a tree. When he cast it into the waters, the waters
> were made sweet." *(Exodus 15:22-25)*

This is a classic example of people having a victim's mentality
and how we easily forget that the Lord makes a way out of no way.

One of the main characteristics of this type behavior is that the
'victim' expects sympathy for all the bad things that they have experienced. They want attention from others because that they have
suffered a lot, even though they did not deserve it. They also want
validation for how brave they were for having gone through so
much and still standing.

The victim plays the blame game. At no point will the victim
take responsibility for what they've going through. They shift the
blame onto others and hold them responsible for all their misfor-

tunes and troubles. Here are some examples of 'blame game' thinking and their solutions:

> *"At the end of the day, you are solely responsible for your success and your failure. And the sooner you realize that, you accept that, and integrate that into your work ethic, you will start being successful. As long as you blame others for the reason you aren't where you want to be, you will always be a failure."* --**Erin Cummings**

> *"All blame is a waste of time. No matter how much fault you find with another, and regardless of how much you blame him, it will not change you. The only thing blame does is to keep the focus off you when you are looking for... reasons to explain your unhappiness or frustration."* --**Casey Stengel**

> *"We are taught you must blame your father, your sisters, your brothers, the school, the teachers - but never blame yourself. It's never your fault. But it's always your fault, because if you wanted to change, you're the one who has got to change."* --**Katharine Hepburn**

> *"We are admonished in scripture, "And do not be conformed to this world, but be transformed by the renewing of your mind, that you may prove what is that good and acceptable and perfect will of God."* **(Romans 12:2, NKJV)**

The optimum phrase in this scripture is "the renewing of your mind." The mind (*i.e.*, the mental faculties, reason, or understanding) is, in itself, neutral. When influenced by an evil principle, it becomes an instrument of evil; when influenced by the Spirit, it is an instrument of good. The information with which we supply our minds determines how we respond to life's situations. Your mind is programmable. It is like a computer; sometimes a virus can attack the hard drive and infect its files. Whenever we foster a victim's mindset, negative thoughts to infect our mind and control responses to adversity. Rather than thinking like a victim, think like a winner!

Life is the sum total of choices and their consequences. We all have said at one time or another that we don't have anything to prove to people. That statement is partially valid; however, we have something to prove to God. For Christians, winning in life is the offspring of a mind developed and sustained by the Word of God and the Holy Spirit's influence.

"You will keep him in perfect peace, whose mind is stayed on You..." **(Isaiah 26:3, NKJV)**

Another prominent sign displayed by a person with a victim's mentality is playing the self-pity role. The individual believes that life has dealt them an unfair hand and they're constantly seen lamenting with questions like "Why me?". This person believes that others have luckier, happier, and better lives. They are convinced that they are suffering more than anyone else. The say things like, "Other people are more blessed than me!" They think life isn't fair because God is unfair or perhaps God has forgotten about them. Some people find themselves trying to self-medicate with drugs, sex, overeating, shopping, or self-destructive behavior. More often than not, the vicious cycle continues from childhood to adulthood.

Victims develop a tendency of pity themselves due to lack of confidence and low self-esteem. They are known to use terms like, "I can't" (negating one's ability) or "I must" (having no choice) common. Victims tend to demonstrate self-harming ways. They refuse to analyze their actions and thereby fail to improve. So, the spiral of destructive thinking perpetuates and limits their ability to win. Instead, not only do they become defensive and dismiss suggestions, they also develop a negative opinion about anyone who suggests change. Over time their self-esteem suffers, and winning in life's battles becomes increasingly difficult. It's important to note that one of the most difficult things in life is to build self-esteem. I believe all of us, no matter what level of upbringing, have been exposed to conditions that have damaged our self-esteem or self-worth to some extent. Some situations were beyond our control. In order to win, "victims" must decide that they are going to rise up above any challenge. This is only possible, however, with God's help and direction.

Of course, I realize some situations are worse than others. Nevertheless, it is very important we learn how fight in this faith walk. We must walk by faith and not by sight. We can't be moved by what we see or hear, and we certainly can't be driven by our fears.

"For God hath not given us the spirit of fear; but of power, and of love, and of a sound mind." (2 Timothy 1:7)

We are not debtors to our broken past, neither are we to glorify our painful past.

"Therefore, brethren, we are debtors — not to the flesh, to live according to the flesh. For if you live according to the flesh you will die; but if by the Spirit you put to death the deeds of the body, you will live. For as many as are led by the Spirit of God, these are sons of God. For you did not receive the spirit of bondage again to fear, but you received the Spirit of adoption by whom we cry out, "Abba, Father." **(Romans 8:12-15)**

Growing up as a child, I thought of myself as the black sheep in my family. That way of thinking perpetuated into my early adult life. It was fueled by the longing for my biological father, who unfortunately was not in my life as a child and most of my adult life. Even though God was doing great things in my life, I secretly carried the emotional pain. I remember the many nights I woke up in the middle of the night with tears rolling down my face. Many times, we struggle emotionally in private while trying to hold it together publicly because of the calling on our lives. During this same time I was juggling my marriage, fathering my three daughters, and overseeing my ministry. I was working a full-time job, going to night school, and doing other things on the side to make ends meet. My life was a mental juggling act. The battle was real! I literally felt like I was about to lose my mind. I prayed and asked God to set me free from the pain and lift my mind out of this broken place. Our heavenly Father takes pride in assisting us in winning over the victim's mentality. Through the power of prayer and they Holy Spirit, He delivered me with a mighty hand. One day I said to the Lord, "I am tired and ready for deliverance." He said to me, "When you confess to Me that you are sick, I will heal you." Immediately, I opened my mouth and confessed my sickness, and immediately, He healed me. Today, I celebrate the victory over a victim's mentality.

"Therefore, if anyone is in Christ, he is a new creation; old things have passed away; behold, all things have become new." (2 Corinthians 5:17)

I want to share another time I had to battle a victim's mindset. In 2016, I purchased a tax franchise. I researched the company's background and for the most part, everything seemed to be in good standing. I even hired an attorney to investigate the company. After everything was confirmed to be okay I moved forward with the personal training, which included buying all the necessary supplies and training my staff. I was excited about the potential income generation and the fact that I was going to help people to live a better life. I hired several tax preparers and planned to bless my church with thousands of dollars. I just knew that this was the moment I had been praying about. After many attempts to succeed in business, I believed this was it. Lo and behold, tax season came. I was confident that I would witness the manifestation of the vision coming to pass. After weeks of working, what I anxiously expected just did not happen. The outcome fell way short of what I believed God for. When tax season was over, I struggled emotionally and psychologically. I was disappointed to the tenth power. My conversation with God about the faith and works processes, however, gave me a new hope. He reminded me about walking by faith and not by sight. I didn't allow the victim's mentality to keep me down. Instead, I decided to regroup and strategize a new vision. When you know you are born to win, you get up and get back in the fight.

*"The hand of the diligent will rule." **(Proverbs 12:24, NKJV)***

PREPARE THE PATH FOR VICTORY

5

Having a clear path to victory is the first step to winning. Please understand the lens to see winning may become cloudy as a result of the obstacles in front of you. A winner, however, cannot be deterred from moving forward because of what they see ahead. As a matter of fact, challenges and distractions will accompany every battle. The better we are prepared, the greater the potential to win. I remember coach Nick Saban stating he was going to give his team a few days to celebrate after he and the University of Alabama football team won the 2017 National Championship. He limited the team's time to celebrate because he didn't want them to suffer from the complacency of winning. The strategy with this type of thinking was to help them understand preparation is not for the past, but for the future. In order to win, you have to plan for the next battle. Failing to plan is a plan to fail. Even though things may not go as planned, not having a plan is unacceptable.

When I think about preparation, I think about vision. Vision is an idea of where you desire to be over time. It is a mental picture of a future state and what you would like to achieve. You may have short- and long-range plans; however, the vision provides guidance and inspiration.

Inspiring a shared vision is an important part of effective, transformational leadership and organizational success. Visions are not accomplished without strategy, accountability, discipline, execution, and momentum. These terms are synonymous with preparation. The very essence of preparation is to arrange or prepare something for use. Preparation cannot happen without vision. Where are you going? What do you hope to achieve? Who is your target audience? What is your product? What resources are available? What does my team look like? Without vision, the battle or contest will fail or be lost miserably. The scripture below teaches us,

*"Where there is no vision the people perish." (**Proverbs 29:18**)*

Every vision has four essential building blocks. The first one is "Confidence". It is paramount that we believe in ourselves. Merriam Webster defines the term "confidence" as "a feeling or belief that you can do something well or succeed at something." Confidence is the belief in your own abilities. It is the self-assurance or belief in your ability to succeed. Believing in yourself is another foundational component of learning. If you don't believe in yourself, growing and learning will be hard. I have an "I can do it" attitude. I have discovered I am my number one cheerleader in life.

"A man cannot be comfortable without his own approval" --**Mark Twain**

"Self-confidence is the first requisite to great undertakings." --**Samuel Johnson**

Like knowledge, confidence can't be transferred. It's not about motivation, tenacity, or drive. It's about **YOU** believing that you can do it! You should never feel as if you have to over-explain yourself. You should never have to feel indecisive or second-guess your decisions. You should also not have to modify your behavior based on what others think. Remember: Confidence begins with you, and the Word gives us a roadmap.

"I can do all things through Christ who strengthens me." **(Philippians 4:13)**

"Your life is the fruit of your own doing. You have no one to blame but yourself." --**Joseph Campbell**

Confidence and passion go hand in hand. Passion is fervor. It is obsession, excitement, and enthusiasm. Vision invokes emotion. There is no such thing as an emotionless vision. A clear, focused vision allows us to experience the emotions associated with our anticipated future ahead of time. These emotions serve to reinforce our commitment to the vision. They provide a sneak preview of things to come.

Motivation

The second building block to vision is "Motivation". Vision-driven people are motivated people. Find me a man or woman who lacks motivation and I will show you someone with little or no vision. Ideas, yes; dreams, maybe; vision, not a chance! The lack of vision is the reason many people never finish anything. Motivation is what gets us out of the bed in the morning when the burdens of life weigh us down. It is the driving force that pushes us toward our vision. When you are motivated, you are driven and more determined to create the life that you want to live. You don't suddenly believe that everything in life is easy, but you are prepared to do whatever it takes to achieve your goals, regardless of the challenges posed.

Perhaps you are unhappy with life and feel stuck in a rut. One thing is for sure: If you do what you have always done, you will always end up in the same place. As Albert Einstein argued, insanity is doing the same thing repeatedly while expecting a different result. The desire to change is one of the most important factors in goal-setting, but it is not enough to have that desire just once. Desire for change must be maintained through the process, and that is what motivation really is. Motivation is one of the most important factors in determining how much success you achieve.

Motivation is important for several reasons. First, motivation is the driving force for identifying and setting goals. Goals come from an innate desire to change something in your life. The second reason is prioritization. Whatever you want to achieve in life, you need to commit to it and focus energy on it. Prioritization helps you to target and focus on the most important tasks. Thirdly, motivation drives action. Anybody can draw up a plan, but it's value will never be known until you put it into action. Setting a goal is not enough to achieve it. You need to take consistent, decisive, and effective action to bring it into reality.

Why is taking action important? Everyone wants to live a comfortable life. They want peaceful relationships, their own home and car, and enough money to vacation and live comfortably. To have all of this as just a dream or plan isn't enough. What is required is action! Action can thrust you forward and move you closer to the things you desire. Without any action, you remain stale and stagnant

Taking action can be difficult and challenging; however, taking the first step to move out of your comfort zone is the only way to begin the journey toward your desired destination. No matter how small the step, the most important thing is to move! l Move towards your dream and vision. No matter how knowledgeable and intelligent you are, no matter how much faith you have in God, if you do not take action based on what you know, you will never experience success or accomplish your goals.

In the Bible, a great lesson about motivation and action, is through the woman who had a flow of blood for twelve years.

"When she heard about Jesus, she came behind Him in the crowd and touched His garment. For she said, "If only I may touch His clothes, I shall be made well." (Mark 5:27-28, NKJV)

I can only imagine the psychological, emotional, and physical state with which she was challenged in her condition. Her motivation to be healed moved her to action. She took the risk and the first step by pressing through the crowd and touching Jesus. Her willingness to take action exposed her to an experience that changed her life forever.

Overcoming Setbacks

The third building block is "Overcoming Setbacks." I don't know of a time in my life when I didn't have setbacks. A setback is defined as something that reverses or delays the progress of somebody or something. Roadblocks are obstacles that do a little bit more than just slow you down. They're more like tar paper. They threaten to make and keep you stuck. Setbacks are usually relatively minor "hiccups," in that they don't stop you. They're more like speed bumps–they simply slow you down. Think of them as a problem that makes your progress harder or success less likely. Your relationship with God, and your marriage, finances, career, ministry, parenting, etc. will have setbacks. Every successful person, the ones we tend to look to for inspiration, has faced their fair share of setbacks before, during, and after achieving something great. Setbacks can work for and against us. It really boils down to one's attitude in the moment.

Maybe you planned to have a project completed by Friday, but something happened and you couldn't finish it until Monday. Perhaps you completely missed the deadline. Make peace with yourself and realize that things are going to happen. Steve Jobs' story is a perfect example. He cofounded Apple (which was Macintosh at the time) at the age of 21, becoming a millionaire within two short years. A few years later, after having a disagreement with the company's cofounder, the board decided to remove him from position at Apple, essentially firing him from the company he helped create. This led to a midlife crisis, in which Jobs thought of all his other career options. He went on to create two more successful companies (NeXT and Pixar) before returning to Apple (which was floundering after he left). So, even though he once found himself without a job, he was able to turn things around by creating his own opportunities. He didn't allow the initial setback with Apple to define or determine his destiny. He didn't make excuses, he made adjustments. Then, he went on to lead Apple to its position as a leading global tech firm. The main thing is never make an excuse for not getting the job done. Excuses are what the uncommitted offer when they are not committed to winning.

"If you live life long enough, you'll make mistakes. But, if you learn from them, you'll be a better person. It's how you handle adversity, not how it affects you. The main thing is never quit, never quit, never quit." --William Clinton

"You may encounter many defeats, but you must not be defeated. In fact, it may be necessary to encounter the defeats, so you can know who you are, what you can rise from, how you can still come out of it." --Maya Angelou

"If you can't fly then run, if you can't run then walk, if you can't walk then crawl, but whatever you do, you have to keep moving forward." --Martin Luther King, Jr.

Clear Direction

The fourth building block to vision is Clear Direction. You're proud of your new vision statement. It sounds nice, even inspiring, but the vision is useless unless it can direct action. Your vision lays out a destination; your destination guides your strategy; and strategy chooses action. It's action that leads to success. In those moments of action, having clear direction is crucial for building momentum. It is one thing to determine where you want to go and another thing to know how you want to get there.

Whether playing in a basketball game, building a brand or business, we are always moving (forward, backward, or in circles). Most of us would, I imagine, want to move forward -- achieving something (i.e. becoming fitter, stronger, wealthier, more skillful or happier). Yet, so many of us get stuck in a rut going over the same ground like a mouse in a wheel, recycling indecision and procrastination. The most practical advantage of a vision is to set direction for our lives. Having clear direction serves as a roadmap. Vision simplifies decision making, while having clear direction moves us toward realizing the vision. Anything that moves us toward the realization of our vision gets a green light. With clear direction, the vision is made plain. We are instructed in scripture to write the vision and make it plain or simple. The more we can simplify the path we want to take, the greater the potential of the vision coming to pass. Nothing is wrong with seeing the big picture. As a matter of fact, seeing the big picture is extremely important. Something is wrong, however, when we have uncertainties about how we are going to accomplish the vision that comprises the big picture. Vision allows you to move purposefully in a predetermined direction.

Purpose

The fifth building block to vision is Purpose. Purpose is why we do what we do. "Why" is a small word; however, it is the birthing canal and the highway that leads to seeing success in every area of lives. Without a 'why', our desire and vision are dead on arrival. Your 'why' is your reason for not giving up when the odds of losing or failing were greater than the odds of winning. It is the reason that perpetuates the passion to fight through pain and suffering to overcome and win. I believe when a person fails to define their 'why', not only do they fail in life, but inevitably they also fail to discover their purpose. Unfortunately, many have succumbed to thinking that earning more money, and gaining more earthly material or people will produce peace and happiness. These things will not suffice when it comes to discovering purpose. People who know their purpose know who they are, what they are, and why they are.

Have you ever thought about what your purpose is in life? Some of us live our entire lives trying to figure out the purpose of our existence. Some people fail and some succeed, but some know their purpose and still divert from it. When you know your purpose, you tend to live a more meaningful existence than those who don't. You tend to live each day to the fullest because you know who you are, where you come from, and where you're going. Purpose helps you stay focused. When you know your purpose, focusing on what matters the most becomes easier. By focusing on a particular goal, it's easier to find your direction and avoid distractions. Too often, we get pulled in so many directions trying figure out which way to go, who to connect with, establishing career goals, and so on. Knowing your purpose helps to find your true passion, and passion becomes an important driver to achieve something extraordinary.

Whether it is a childhood dream or a new opportunity, passion will push you to reach your goals. People who know their purpose are unstoppable. They are true to their purpose and allow it to shape their life accordingly. As matter of fact, everything in their life revolves around purpose. People who don't know their purpose are unclear about what they want; therefore, they waste time on futile things. In many instances, they spend their entire lives in what I call purpose obscurity. Purpose obscurity is a state of not knowing your purpose.

It is defined as an unfulfilled life and a feeling of emptiness. Sadly, many people end up trying to self-medicate or succumb to a lesser version of God's design or plan for their lives. When you understand your purpose, you're able to constantly express it and will make decisions based on thoughts, feelings and actions around it. A person who knows their purpose tends to make a greater impact through their work, which encourages a feeling of gratification. With purpose comes values, which are an integral aspect of a person's life. Values are the rules that guide decisions and help define goals. Knowing your purpose helps you live life with integrity.

People who know their purpose know who they are, what they are, and why they are. And when you know yourself, living a life that's true to your core values becomes easier. Core values are what tells us when we're on the right path and helps us find and connect with others sharing similar views of the world.

As a man of God, my relationship with God and passionate desire to please Him have become the umpire in my life. I have learned when I let Him make the calls in my life, they helps to govern my life by Godly convictions. I don't always agree with the calls He makes; however, because I understand purpose, I know it is working together for my success. I remember when I acknowledged my calling to preach the Gospel, outside of accepting Jesus Christ as my personal Lord and Savior. It was the second-most supernatural, life-changing experience in my life. It ignited a fire in me that has been burning for over thirty-five years. Suddenly, I realized my purpose. It became the launching pad and catalyst for not only direction for my destiny, but also an internal compass that began to unfold and impact every area of my life. Every human who avoids and perhaps refuses to pursue God is not only aborting their peace, but their God- given purpose and destiny. I have learned that I can't win the contest of life without God being in the center. Life is like a fading wind without Him defining my life. It is just a matter of time when the wind will stop blowing.

Always remember vision translates into purpose. A vision gives you reason to get up in the morning. If you don't show up, you won't accomplish something important. You matter! You matter a lot! Without you, what could be or what should be –won't be! Vision is an important link between current reality and the future.

*"You can only become truly accomplished at something you love. Don't make money your goal. Instead pursue the things you love doing, and then do them so well that people can't take their eyes off of you." -- **Maya Angelou***

THE POWER OF EXECUTION

6

As a visionary, I will admit that I have found myself asking many times, why haven't I completed certain tasks or what was in my heart to do. The hard truth is we are all guilty of starting strong, but not finishing. One of the things that frustrates me exponentially, is to have a great meeting or training and nothing happens afterwards. The number one reason things don't get done is poor execution.

Once again, for the record, we are all guilty of it at some point or another. Many times, we leave a trail of broken commitments and unfinished goals. Every January, people declare the new year is going to be different. They make goals based on certain events in life, only to find themselves stuck and repeating the same behavior. Does this sound like you? Unlearning bad habits is very difficult, but it can be done with the right approach.

Execution is the single most important trait of a successful person, for acting outweighs talking. Successful people not only know that, but they also live by it every day. The perfect plan, poorly executed, will fail; however, a lousy plan, well executed, is often successful. As obvious as it may seem, often, the way to fix a failure is simple: work harder. If you fail to lose weight on a diet, is your diet the problem? Or, is the problem inconsistent follow-through? May I suggest in most cases the diet is not the problem, but perhaps the lack of commitment to working harder.

Whenever I get stuck on a goal, my first response is always to work harder. Often, the plan I already have will work, the only thing needed is to just apply more effort towards it. I realize the biggest factor in my success or failure won't be which method used. What matters most is whether I work hard enough for it; if I'm going beyond the effort threshold. One thing I know about champions is they understand the harder they work and the more pain they can endure increases their chances of winning exponentially. Every goal has a minimum work threshold. If you don't invest minimal effort, failure is inevitable. Success is dependent on effort. Sometimes more effort is needed if the plan is weak.

Many people fail in life as a result of poor or a lack of implementation -- not vision. A person can have a great vision, but fall short because of poor execution. Execution is carrying out or putting into effect a plan, order, or course of action. Keep in mind that most of today's successful entrepreneurs simply out-executed those who created the original idea. We can have a great strategy and a carefully devised plan of action to achieve our goals; however, without execution it is like having a body void of without muscular strength.

"A lot of organizations put great strategies together, but they don't follow through. Ninety-percent of them fail at the execution part of the strategy." (**quote source**)

Strategy is deciding what to do. Execution is all about making something happen. The follow- through is important. The most essential components of execution are thinking, planning and acting. Thinking is defined as the forming of thoughts. It creates the mental picture, and non-physical narrative or mental description of the contest or plan. It initiates the first step toward the planned outcome. Before I participate in any competitive or non-competitive platform, I spend a lot of time incubating my thoughts as I contemplate the execution process. This mental process includes seeing myself having what I need to win.

Sometimes, you cannot not win by yourself or with limited resources. That is when you consider who you need on your team to help advance your goals. I remember when I wrote my first book and how excited. I was when I finished it. The excitement quickly dissipated, however, when I realized I didn't execute a well thought- out strategy. For instance, I did not take a few things into consideration. I did not identify my target audience. I also didn't utilize the various advertising or social media platforms available, and neither did I have a web site. Of course, there is more to the process. Consequently, I did not maximize the moment. In my estimation I experienced little success.

I cannot over-emphasize the power of thinking when it comes to winning. I call this process The Psychology of Winning. The essence of the word "psychology" is mindset or attitude. Your attitude is your mental position or posture. I have found myself stuck in transition mentally. I had to realize that if I didn't change my way of thinking, nothing was going to change for me.

Too often leaders, including pastors, businessmen, and team leaders, get trapped in transition because they're unable to mentally shift in their head to see what is in their hearts come to pass. Execution starts in the mind first. Before planning can begin, you must see the big picture in your thought process. The optimum word is "see", meaning using your imagination to create a mental picture of what winning looks like. I understand this can be very difficult, particularly if you spend most of your days fighting against the odds of success. I spent many days questioning m y process. In some cases I wondered if I should have done things differently, or if I missed God, perhaps. With all the lingering questions, I had to conquer my fears and doubts and continue to activate my imagination to see what I hoped for.

Champions have an innate ability to see victory in every situation. I asked a professional golfer about making a successful shot. He stated that every professional golfer imagines what the shot will look like before he takes it. In other words, he forms the shot in his mind first and then tries to make what he saw a reality.

To further validate the point, my wife and I have been married over forty years. We have seen some good and bad days. One thing is for sure: Every marriage will be tried in the fire. We have gone to marriage retreats, workshops, and bootcamps; and we have prayed and fasted. We are both born-again Christians who love Jesus. We have ministered on various platforms, teaching other couples marriage principles. Without question, we have been given the tools to have a successful marriage. We have learned, however, that without applying the tools and changing our way of thinking, we would not be married today. Trust me, it is a work in progress. To God be all the glory!

Having a plan is equally important to proper execution. I have already stated in this book that if we fail to plan, we plan to fail. Winning is not an involuntary act of our will, it is a voluntary one. A vision without a plan is like a life with no direction or purpose. The human body is comprised of twelve different organ systems, and each has a specific role to play. Each organ is intrinsically connected to another. Their functionality is fundamental to the health and success of the human body. If one of the organs fail to function according its purpose, the others are impacted negatively. Likewise, understanding the necessity of having a plan to execute is vitally important to winning. Passion is essential to achieving goals; however, not having a plan to channel that passion will lead to disappointment.

How many times have you started or bought something only to discover, later down the road, you didn't do a very good job planning? I remember when I purchased my first nice used car. I was so excited because it was a step above all the other hoopties I purchased. I calculated how much I could afford to pay monthly on the note and insurance; however, I failed to include maintenance costs (i.e. oil changes, new tires, mechanical issues, etc.). As a result of my failed plan, I found myself scrambling to keep my car running when an issue arose while, at the same time, maintaining the monthly note. You can see how important planning is in executing your vision.

Now that you have given thought to vision and established a plan of action, now it's time to act. Action is the mother of execution. Without it, nothing happens. Action is the process of doing something in order to achieve a purpose. The Bible states, "Faith without works is dead." You can have all the faith in the world, but you can't experience what you expect until you put it into action. You cannot experience victory without a battle and a championship without a contest.

"If you don't know where you're going, any road will get you there."
– Lewis Carroll

One sure way to act on an established vision or plan is to set deadlines. Winners in any arena understand the importance of establishing action boundaries. While we may not like it our behavior changes when someone gives us a deadline. Simply setting deadlines for goals and objectives goes a long way toward achieving them! Meeting deadlines ensures reliability and respect. People prefer to conduct business with those who are highly believed and known for their overall sense of integrity and loyalty. Determining priorities is crucial to establishing a specific plan of action. I have learned that people will pull you in one-hundred different directions if you allow them. We can become so busy helping and aiding others in their goals that we neglect to establish our own.

An effective plan of action should include accountability. To be accountable means to be subject to giving an account or having the obligation to report, explain, or justify something to someone else. If you bring up the word "accountability", you're bound to get a reaction. The type of response you get will reveal a lot about the responder's heart and where they are in life. The very idea of ac-countability is counter-intuitive to our natural selfishness and pride; therefore, it's not something we love naturally.

Accountability means answering or accounting for actions and results. We increase our winning potential substantially when we hold ourselves accountable for our plan. If you simply have an idea or goal, you've already beat the odds. Consciously deciding to achieve something increases your chances from ten to twenty-five percent. Once you determine priorities and timelines, your chances of succeeding increase to fifty percent. When you commit to someone that you will do it, the probability of success increases to sixty-five percent. Moreover, when you include accountability partners, the odds are in your favor: ninety-five percent.

"Accountability breeds response-ability." *--****Stephen Covey***

Another path to accountability is having an accountability partner to push plan execution. An accountability partner is some-one who coaches another to help them keep a commitment. They help us to stay on track or get back on track. They can uncover blind spots, be a good sound board, and even assist in keeping us grounded.

Sometimes people become comfortable disappointing themselves and breaking their own commitments. But when you have someone on your side, rooting for, encouraging, and reminding you of your plan, you're less likely to give up. You don't want to disappoint them.

While writing this book, I can't help but think of my oldest daughter, Leandra. Through her pushing and encouragement, I started live posts on Facebook and established the "Real Talk with The Bishop" brand. Initially, I resisted because of my already extremely busy schedule. She was relentless in her encouragement, to say the least. I finally started the process, not knowing that the platform would expose my ministry to literally thousands of viewers worldwide. Also, it launched the platform for this book. In addition, Facebook selected me as a Brand Collabs Manager", which allows me to partner on brand deals and earn money by creating and sharing content with followers and advertisers. This narrative is a clear picture of "The Power of Execution." King Solomon said,

> "He becomes poor who works with a slack and idle hand, but the hand of the diligent makes rich." (Proverbs 10:4, AMP)

DEVELOPING A CHAMPIONS MINDSET IN THE FACE OF ADVERSITY

7

The launching pad for winning starts in our mind and with our emotions. The tougher we are mentally and emotionally, the better we perform under pressure.

> *"Pressure can burst a pipe or pressure can make a diamond."* -- **Robert Horry**

Mental Toughness

Mental toughness is a huge indicator of success. We all reach critical points in our lives when our mental toughness is tested. It might be because of toxic friendships or colleagues, a dead-end job, struggling relationship, or, perhaps, a failing business. Whatever the challenge, you must be strong, see things through a new lens, and take decisive action if you want to move through it successfully.

We all want good friends, good jobs, and good relationships. It sounds easy, but it isn't.

It's hard to be mentally tough, especially when you feel stuck. The ability to break the mold and take a bold new direction requires that extra grit, daring, and spunk that only the mentally toughest people have. How the mentally tough set themselves apart from the crowd is fascinating. Where others see impenetrable barriers, they see challenges to overcome. As a matter of fact, they are at their best when challenged. I discovered moments in life when my mind and emotions were being pushed to the limit. During those times, I learned to fight my way out of difficult situations as my faith in God was being tested.

Mentally tough people subscribe to Ford's notion that your mentality has a powerful effect on your ability to succeed. This notion isn't just a motivational tool, it's a fact. A recent study at the University of Melbourne showed that confident people progress to earn higher wages and get promotions more quickly than others. True confidence, as opposed to false confidence, projects itself in masked insecurities and has its own look. Mentally tough people have an upper hand over the doubtful and skittish because their confidence inspires others and helps them to make things happen. Mental toughness is a measure of individual resilience and confidence that may predict success in sports, education, and the workplace. It is the ability to resist, manage, and overcome doubts, worries, concerns, and circumstances that prevent you from succeeding or excelling at a what you set out to achieve.

When a person is mentally tough, they are flexible and constantly able to adapt. They know that fear of change is paralyzing and a major threat to success and happiness. They look for change lurking around the corner, and form a plan of action should those changes occur. Only when you embrace change can you find the good in it. You need to have an open arm and mind if you're going to recognize and capitalize on the opportunities that change creates.

As I state previously, we are bound to fail when we keep doing the same things we've always done in the hope that ignoring change will make it go away. After all, insanity is doing the same thing repeatedly while expecting a different result. Research conducted at the University of California in San Francisco showed that the more difficulty you have saying "No", the more likely you are to experience stress, burnout, and even depression. Mentally tough people know that saying "No" is healthy, and they have the self-esteem and foresight to make their no's clear. When it's time to say "No", mentally tough people avoid phrases such as, "I don't think I can", "I'm not certain", "I might be able to", or "I will get back with you." They're able to say "No" with confidence because it honors their existing commitments and ensures the opportunity to successfully fulfill them.

The mentally tough also know how to exert self-control. They say "No" to themselves. They delay gratification and avoid impulsive actions that cause harm. In Genesis, we see a great biblical narrative that gives credence to this point. Joseph choose not to succumb to the pressure of Potiphar's wife's sexual advancement.

> *"From the day Joseph was put in charge of his master's household and property, the Lord began to bless Potiphar's household for Joseph's sake. All his household affairs ran smoothly, and his crops and livestock flourished. So, Potiphar gave Joseph complete administrative responsibility over everything he owned. With Joseph there, he didn't worry about a thing—except what kind of food to eat! Joseph was a very handsome and well-built young man, and Potiphar's wife soon began to look at him lustfully. 'Come and sleep with me,' she demanded. But Joseph refused. 'Look,' he told her, 'my master trusts me with everything in his entire household. No one here has more authority than I do. He has held back nothing from me except you, because you are his wife. How could I do such a wicked thing? It would be a great sin against God.'"* **(Genesis 39:5-9, NLT)**

The story goes on to tell that Potiphar's wife falsely accused Joseph of trying to sleep with her and had him put him in prison But because of his commitment to God and mental fortitude to maintain his integrity, he became the governor of all of Egypt.

As a leader and pastor, I have been challenged to make tough decisions. I remember when I was faced with the decision to close our daycare and school after fifteen years of existence because of declining enrollment. I wrestled with the decision for months. I thought about how long they were in existence, all the hard work and prayer that went into seeing the vision come to pass, my staff and their well-being, and how closing both would affect them financially. I thought of their commitment to the vision for so many years and found myself stressing over the pressing reality. The deal breaker was when making payroll became increasingly difficult. It was emotionally draining every time I thought about it. At the same time, I was pastoring a demanding church. By the way, I forget to mention I was haunted by the potential of public embarrassment and scrutiny from the people who were waiting on my fail.

There are times in life when we find ourselves in difficult, pressing situations in which the mental pressure is overwhelming. I realized I had to remove emotion from the equation and make a tough decision. I was either going to press forward under the current circumstances or close our daycare and school. I choose to close them because the financial odds were against me.

Emotional Intelligence

Another key component to "Developing A Champions Mindset in the Face of Adversity" is "Emotional Intelligence." Emotional intelligence is the cornerstone of mental toughness. You cannot be mentally tough without the ability to fully understand and tolerate strong, negative emotions and do something productive with them. Some of the characteristics of Emotional Intelligence are Self-awareness, Self-management, Self-regulation; Self-motivation, and an ability to build relationships empathically. Emotional Intelligence and our ability to draw on it as a reserve, help us by assisting in looking after our physical and mental health and well-being. It's a driver of success, as we are better able to effectively manage relationships and resolve conflicts. Emotions can be either liabilities or assets, depending on how we manage them. God designed emotions to be gauges, not guides. They're meant to report to you, not dictate to you. The pattern of your emotions will give you a reading on where your hope is because they are wired into what you believe and value. They reveal the magnitude of what your heart loves, trusts, and fears.

Moments that test mental toughness are ultimately testing emotional intelligence (EI). Unlike your IQ, which is fixed, your EI is a flexible skill that can be improved upon with understanding and effort. I understand why ninety percent of top performers have high EIs. Emotional intelligence manifests both in personal competence (self-awareness and self-management) and in social competence (social awareness and relationship management). People with high EIs are usually the top performers in their organizations. Our physical and psychological responses to emotions may start with the fight-or flight syndrome and then escalate. According to the Center for Creative Leadership, seventy-five percent of careers are *"derailed for reasons related to emotional competencies, including the inability to handle interpersonal problems, unsatisfactory team leadership during times of difficulty or conflict, or inability to adapt to change or elicit trust"*. Perhaps they are right.

Organizations now are requiring potential employees to take EI tests. Why is emotional intelligence important in the workplace?

The significance of emotional intelligence is best reflected through employee performance. Emotional intelligence can identify both the biases and clarity in thinking patterns that allow an individual to make sound decisions. In other words, emotional intelligence can lead to better business decisions. Emotionally intelligent employees are more likely to remain calm under pressure. Those with high EI are also better at resolving conflicts. Whether connecting with others and improving interpersonal communication, achieving success in the workplace or social relationships, dealing with stress and improving motivation, or refining decision-making skills – emotional intelligence plays a central role in realizing success both personally and professionally.

Personal competence is the ability to stay aware of your emotions and manage your behavior and tendencies. Self-Awareness is your ability to accurately perceive emotions and stay aware of them as they happen. On "Real Talk With the Bishop" I taught a series titled, "How to Get Closer to God -Transformed in My Emotional Health." I know that is a long title; nevertheless, the focus was dealing with how you feel. I talked about relationship barriers, one of which was low Emotional Intelligence. A cornerstone to successful relationships is having the ability to monitor emotions (both yours and others) and discern the difference between them.

"If your emotional abilities aren't in hand, if you don't have self-awareness, if you are not able to manage your distressing emotions, if you can't have empathy and have effective relationships, then no mat-

ter how smart you are, you are not going to get very far. **Researcher Daniel Goleman**

Emotional and social intelligence is not only vital in finding success and satisfaction in your career, it's also biblical. Christians should have high levels of EI. I can recall numerous occasions in early ministry when I would go into leadership sessions fully frustrated. Sometimes my voice tone clearly demonstrated that I was upset about how things were going. Please understand, for the most part I am a pretty level-headed guy; however, as I look back, I realize I was undeveloped emotionally to know how to communicate effectively. In my opinion, a low EI is a deal breaker when comes to winning. One of my colleagues told me he had to stop playing basketball because he realized he did not have the emotional balance not to take the game so seriously. Note, he was not a professional basketball player. He was a successful attorney with his own law firm. To his credit, he was able to assess his own EI. It is very important that we get a handle on our emotions and learn how to regulate them in order to maximize our intelligence and skills.

The Bible is full of references to man's emotions and often contrasts wisdom and foolishness.

"A fool gives full vent to his anger, but a wise man holds it in check." **(Proverbs 29:11)**

"Whoever is slow to anger is better than the mighty, and he who rules his spirit than he who takes a city." **Proverbs 16:22**

When the body of Christ is well-adjusted socially and emotionally, others are more inclined to listen to what you have to say.

"Let your light so shine before men, that they may see your good works and glorify your Father in heaven." **(Matthew 5:16, NKJV)**

"Therefore, prepare your minds for action; be self-controlled; set your hope fully on the grace to be given you when Jesus Christ is revealed." **(1 Peter 1:13, NIV)**

Champions See Adversity as an Opportunity to Succeed

One thing all champions have in common is the ability to seize the moment when adversity arises. Adversity is a necessary part of life. Without challenges there are no opportunities to grow, to learn, to develop. In essence, without adversity where is the thrill. Yet many individuals view adversity in a bad light and as a result they are not prepared for when it comes.

Champions accept what they can and cannot control. They do not get hung up on things they are unable to do anything about. For example, when they make mistakes, they can hit the reset button and move forward. They have trained themselves to let adversity come and go, without it negatively impacting their performance. Instead of trying to control the outcomes, or even the past, champions remain focused on their own attitude, effort, and emotional response to things that happen in life. I have learned to accept things I can change and the things I cannot change. Often our best self is lost trying to please everybody, only to discover we fall way short in our attempt. The mind of a champion is one that uses every opportunity in life to win. It might not look like it to everybody else, however we know the victory is not achieve in winning a trophy or plaque, but in our head.

Elite athletes seek out challenges because they represent opportunities to overcome obstacles, to persevere, to achieve something greater; in short, the fun is in the struggle. Challenges bring out a champion's competitive spirit, which in turn brings out the best performances. You will never know how great you can become until you learn how to fight when your back is up against the wall and your hands are tied behind your back. Champions do the next right thing when faced with adversity. Have you ever seen a great player make a mistake? Sure, you have, but watch what they do NEXT. More often than not, elite players find themselves making big plays after poor ones. They move on to the next play and put 100% of themselves into the challenge. Champions do the next right thing, which means putting the past to rest and refocusing on the upcoming opportunity.

According to Psychology Today, "Our attitudes determine whether we'll succeed, or not, according to research led by Dave Collins and published in Frontiers in Psychology. Collins found that the athletes at the top of their sports continually push for improvement, and have deep internal motivation, but they also respond to setbacks and obstacles more positively and proactively. They are more determined when things go haywire. Even in the throes of adversity, they keep working to come back better, stronger, faster." Without question, real champions see every failure and or loss as motivation to prepare for the next opportunity to win.

Everyone suffers adversity, but those who succeed and climb to the top bring a certain resilience, attitude, and perspective that allows them to move on to acquire the knowledge and experience and practice they need to become even better.

WE ALWAYS WIN EVERY TIME!

8

It has been said that you can't win if you don't compete, and you can't compete if you quit. Winning is not a gift, it is a matter of conviction. One's ability to navigate through life's many challenges and maintain a winning attitude is not easy. If they were, everybody would be good at it.

I have discovered winning is more than being married for over forty years. It is more than being a good father or grandfather. It's more than being a successful pastor or a person of influence in the community. It is even more than being good friend. It is knowing that with Christ as the head of my life, I always win. I would love to win all my golf matches or see all my dreams come to pass. It would be wonderful to Having a perfect marriage or experience nothing but bliss in every area of my life would be wonderful, but we all know that is not real life.

Life is the great equalizer. It doesn't discriminate. It has no bias or prejudices. Good people suffer and die. Sometimes the good suffer with the bad. We all face attacks from different sources. Some have suffered at the hands of evil people. It is called life. The question some might ask is how can losing everything you've worked for equate to winning? Or, how does going through a divorce, which almost caused you to lose your mind, equate to winning? Still yet, how does grieving the loss of a loved one have to do with winning? The reality of our situation shouldn't determine the outcome. The most important thing to remember is with Christ, we always win in life.

> "For I fully expect and hope that I will never be ashamed, but that I will continue to be bold for Christ, as I have been in the past. And I trust that my life will bring honor to Christ, whether I live or die. 21 For to me, living means living for Christ, and dying is even better." (Phil 1:20-22, NLT)

Basically, Paul is saying we win while we are living, and we win if we die. In other words, we can't lose with Jesus leading our lives. We always win!

Remember, life is a marathon and not a sprint. It is filled with many roads travelled. No matter which path you took to get where you are in life, it is never too late to start winning. The fact that the good Lord woke you up today is a sure indicator He has great plans for your life.

My goal in writing this book was, first to glorify God (who is truly amazing) and to help people like me, who have been tried in the fire and refuse to quit. In addition, I want to give the readers tools and strategies for winning in every area of their lives.

So, it is time to refocus your thoughts. I will admit firsthand that refocusing your thoughts can be tough work because the mind where behavior changes. You must readjust the old behavior and replace it with new, positive actions or conduct-- and desirable things you enjoy doing and can do consistently every time. Refuse to be misled by old messages. Dismiss deceptive brain messages and do something healthy and productive instead. One consistent way to replace the old behavior is to begin seeing old patterns as simple distractions.

> *"Therefore, if any man be in Christ, he is a new creature: old things are passed away; behold, all things are become new." (2 Cor 5:17)*

> *"So, we have stopped evaluating others from a human point of view. At one time we thought of Christ merely from a human point of view. How differently we know him now! This means that anyone who belongs to Christ has become a new person. The old life is gone; a new life has begun!" (2 Cor 5:16-17, NLT)*

> *"Bad things do happen; I can choose to sit in perpetual sadness; immobilized by the gravity of my loss or I can choose to rise from the pain and treasure the most precious gift I have – Life itself." (Unknown)*

Winning must first begin in the mind. Our minds cannot be transformed without Christ at the very center of it. He is our source and should, therefore, be the main influencer of our mindset and actions. The reality of life is no matter the situation or circum-stance we face, as long as we have Christ "WE ALWAYS WIN!"